'The devil gave the woman a nudge: "Look at that belt full of money peeping out from under the butcher's shirt!"'

JOHANN PETER HEBEL
Born 1760, Basel, The Swiss Confederacy
Died 1826, Schwetzingen, Grand Duchy of Baden

The stories in this selection were mostly first published in
Johann Peter Hebel's *Schatzkästlein des rheinischen Hausfreundes*
in 1811 and are taken from *The Treasure Chest*, chosen and
translated by John Hibberd in 1994.

HEBEL IN PENGUIN CLASSICS
The Treasure Chest

JOHANN PETER HEBEL

How a Ghastly Story was Brought to Light by a Common or Garden Butcher's Dog

Translated by
John Hibberd and Nicholas Jacobs

PENGUIN BOOKS

PENGUIN CLASSICS

UK | USA | Canada | Ireland | Australia
India | New Zealand | South Africa

Penguin Books is part of the Penguin Random House group of companies
whose addresses can be found at global.penguinrandomhouse.com.

Original translation of *The Treasure Chest* first published in Great Britain by Libris 1994
Published in Penguin Books 1995
This selection published in Penguin Classics 2015
003

Translation copyright © John Hibberd, 1994
'The Safest Path' translation copyright © Nicholas Jacobs, 2015

The moral right of the translators has been asserted

Set in 9.5/13 pt Baskerville 10 Pro
Typeset by Jouve (UK), Milton Keynes
Printed in Great Britain by Clays Ltd, St Ives plc

A CIP catalogue record for this book is available from the British Library

ISBN: 978-0-141-39802-0

www.greenpenguin.co.uk

Contents

The Silver Spoon

An officer in Vienna was thinking, 'Just for once I'll dine at the Red Ox,' and into the Red Ox he went. There were regulars there and strangers, important and unimportant people, honest men and rascals such as you'll find anywhere. They were eating and drinking, some a great deal, others little. They talked and argued about this and that, about how it had rained rocks at Stannern in Moravia, for instance, or about Machin who fought the great wolf in France. When the meal was almost over one or two were drinking a small jug of Tokay to round things off, one man was making little balls from bread crumbs as if he were an apothecary making pills, another was fiddling with his knife or his fork or his silver spoon. It was then the officer happened to notice how a fellow in a green huntsman's coat was playing with a silver spoon when it suddenly disappeared up his sleeve and stayed there.

Someone else might have thought, 'It's no business of mine,' and said nothing, or have made a great fuss. The officer thought, 'I don't know who this green spoon-hunter is and what I might let myself in for,' and he kept as quiet as a mouse, until the landlord came to collect his money. But when the landlord came to collect his money the

1

officer, too, picked up a silver spoon, and tucked it through two button holes in his coat, in one and out the other as soldiers sometimes do in war when they take their spoons with them, but no soup. As the officer was paying his bill the landlord was looking at his coat and thinking, 'That's a funny medal this gentleman's wearing! He must have distinguished himself battling with a bowl of cray-fish soup to have got a silver spoon as a medal! Or could it just be one of mine?' But when the officer had paid the landlord he said, without a sign of a smile on his face, 'The spoon's included, I take it? The bill seems enough to cover it.' The landlord said, 'Nobody's tried that one on me before! If you don't have a spoon at home I'll give you a tin one, but you can't have one of my silver spoons!' Then the officer stood up, slapped the landlord on the shoulder and laughed. 'It was only a joke we were hav-ing,' he said, 'that gentleman over there in the green jacket and me! – My green friend, if you give back that spoon you have up your sleeve I'll give mine back too.' When the spoon-hunter saw that he had been caught in the act and that an honest eye had observed his dishonest hand, he thought, 'Better pretend it was a joke,' and gave back his spoon. So the landlord got his property back, and the spoon thief smiled too – but not for long. For when the other customers saw what had happened they set about him with curses and hounded him out of the Holy of Holies and the landlord sent the boots after him with a big stick. But he stood the worthy officer a bottle of Tokay to toast the health of all honest men.

Remember: You must not steal silver spoons!

Remember: Someone will always stand up for what is right.

The Cheap Meal

There is an old saying: The biter is sometimes bit. But the landlord at the Lion in a certain little town was bitten first. He received a well-dressed customer who curtly demanded a good bowl of broth, the best his money would buy. Then he ordered beef and vegetables too for his money. The landlord asked him, all politeness, if he wouldn't like a glass of wine with it. 'Indeed I would,' his guest replied, 'if I can have a good one for my money.' When he had finished, and he enjoyed it all, he took a worn six-kreuzer piece from his pocket and said, 'Here you are, landlord, there's my money!' The landlord said, 'What's this? You owe me a thaler!' The customer answered, 'I didn't ask for a meal for a thaler, but for my money. Here it is. It's all I have. If you gave me too much for it then that's your fault!' It wasn't really such a clever trick. It called only for cheek and a devil-may-care view of the consequences. But the best is yet to come.

'You're an utter villain,' said the landlord, 'and don't

deserve this. But you can have the meal for nothing and take this twenty-four kreuzer bit as well. Just keep quiet about it and go over to my neighbour who keeps the Bear and try the same trick on him!' He said this because he had had a quarrel with his neighbour and resented his success and each was keen to do the other down.

But the artful customer smiled as he took the money he was offered in his one hand and reached carefully for the door with the other, wished the innkeeper good afternoon, and said, 'I went to the Bear first, it was the landlord there who sent me over here!'

So really both of the innkeepers had been tricked; the cunning customer took advantage of their quarrel. Yet he might have also earned a further reward, grateful thanks from both of them, if they had learnt the right lesson from it and had made things up between them. For peace pays, whereas quarrels have to be paid for.

Dinner Outside

We often complain how difficult or impossible it is to get on with certain people. That may of course be true. But many such people are not bad but only strange, and if you got to know them well with all their ins and outs and learnt to deal with them properly, neither too wilfully nor too indulgently, then many of them might easily be brought to their senses. After all, one servant did manage to do that with his master. Sometimes he could do nothing right by him and, as often happens in such situations, was blamed for many things that were not his fault. Thus one day his master came home in a very bad mood and sat down to dinner. The soup was too hot or too cold for him, or neither; no matter, he was in a bad mood! So he picked up the dish and threw it and its contents out of the open window into the yard below. So what do you think the servant did? He didn't hesitate, he threw the meat he was bringing to table down into the yard after the soup, then the bread, the wine, and finally the tablecloth and everything on it, all down into the yard too. 'What the devil do you think you're doing?' said his master angrily and rose threateningly to his feet. But the servant replied quietly and calmly, 'Pardon me if I misunderstood your wishes. I thought you wanted to eat outside today. The air's warm, the sky's blue, and look how lovely the apple blossom is and how happy the bees are sipping at the flowers!' Never again would the soup go out through the window! His master saw he was wrong, cheered up at the sight of the beautiful spring day, smiled to himself at his man's quick thinking, and in his heart he was grateful to him for teaching him a lesson.

The Clever Judge

Not everything that happens in the East is so wrong. We are told the following event took place there. A rich man had been careless and lost a large sum of money sewn up in a cloth. He made his loss known, and in the usual way offered a reward for its return, in this case a hundred thalers. Soon a good honest man came to see him. 'I have found your money,' he said. 'This must be yours.' He had the open look of an upright fellow with a clear conscience, and that was good. The rich man looked happy too, but only at seeing his precious money again. As for his honesty, that we shall see! He counted the money and worked out quickly how he could cheat this man of the promised reward. 'My friend,' he said, 'there were in fact eight hundred thalers sewn up in this cloth. But I can find only seven hundred. So I take it you must have cut open a corner and taken your one hundred thalers' reward. You acted quite properly. I thank you!' That was not good. But we haven't got to the end yet. Honesty is the best policy, and wrongdoing never proves right. The honest man who had found the money and who was less concerned for his reward than for his blameless name protested that he had found the packet just as he handed it over, and had handed over exactly what he had found. In the end they appeared in court. Both of them stuck to their stories, one that eight hundred thalers were sewn up in the cloth, the other that he had left the packet just as he found it and had taken nothing from it. It was hard to know what to do. But the clever judge, who seemed from the outset to recognize the honesty of the one and the bad faith of the other, approached the problem as follows. He had both swear their statements on solemn oath, and then passed the following judgement: 'Since one of you lost eight hundred thalers and the other found a packet containing only seven hundred, the package found by that second party cannot be the one to which the first party has just claim. You, my honest friend, take back the money you found and put it into safe keeping until the person who lost only seven hundred thalers makes himself known. And you I can only advise to be patient until someone says he has found your eight hundred thalers.' That was his judgement, and that was final.

The Artful Hussar

A hussar in the last war knew that the farmer he met on the road had just sold his hay for a hundred guilders and was on his way home with the money. So he asked him for something to buy tobacco and brandy. Who knows, he might have been happy with a few coppers. But the farmer swore black and blue he had spent his last kreuzer in the nearby village and had nothing left. 'If we weren't so far from my quarters,' said the hussar, 'we could both be helped out of this difficulty; but you have nothing, and neither have I; so we'll just have to go to Saint Alphonsus! We'll share what he gives us like brothers.' This Saint Alphonsus stood carved from stone in an old, little frequented chapel in the fields. At first the farmer was not too keen to make the pilgrimage. But the hussar allowed no objection, and on the way he was so vigorous in his assurances that Saint Alphonsus had never let him down when in need that the farmer began to cherish hopes himself. So you think the hussar's comrade and accomplice was hiding in the deserted chapel, do you? Not a bit of it! No one was there, only the stone figure of Alphonsus, and they knelt before him, and the hussar appeared to be praying fervently. 'This is it!' he whispered to the farmer, 'the saint has just beckoned to me.' He got to his feet and went to put his ear to the lips of stone and came back delighted. 'He's given me a guilder, he says it's in my purse!' And indeed to the other's amazement the hussar took out a guilder, but one that he had had there all the time, and shared it like a brother as promised. That made sense to the farmer and he agreed that the hussar should try again. All went just as before. This time the hussar was even happier when he came back to the farmer. 'Now Saint Alphonsus has given us a hundred guilders all in one go! They're in your purse.' The farmer turned deadly white when he heard this and repeated his protests that he had no money at all. But the hussar persuaded him he must trust Saint Alphonsus and just take a look; Alphonsus had never deceived him! So whether he liked it or not he had to turn his pockets inside out and empty them. Then the hundred guilders appeared all right, and since he had taken half of the hussar's guilder it was no use pleading and imploring, he had to share his hundred.

That was all very artful and cunning, but that doesn't make it right, especially in a chapel.

The Dentist

Two loafers who had been roaming around the country together for some time because they were too lazy to work or had learnt no trade finally got into a tight corner because they had no money left, and they saw no quick way of getting any. Then they had this idea: they went begging at doors for bread which they intended to use, not to fill their stomachs, but to stage a trick. For they kneaded and rolled it into little balls and coated them with the dust from old, rotten worm-eaten wood so that they looked just like yellow pills from the chemist. Then for a couple of pence they bought some sheets of red paper at the bookbinder's (for a pretty colour often helps take people in). Next they cut up the paper and wrapped the pills in it, six or eight to a little packet. Then one of them went on ahead to a village where there was a fair and into the Red Lion where he hoped to find a good crowd. He ordered a glass of wine, but he didn't drink it but sat sadly in a corner holding his face in his hand, moaning under his breath and fidgeting and turning this way and that. The good farmers and townsfolk in the inn thought the poor fellow must have terrible toothache. Yet what could they do? They pitied him, they consoled him, saying it would soon go away, then went back to their drinks and their market-day affairs. Meanwhile the other idler came in. The two scoundrels pretended they had never seen each other in their lives before. They didn't look at each other until the one seemed to react to the other's moans in the corner. 'My friend,' he said, 'have you got toothache?' and he strode slowly over to him. 'I am Dr Schnauzius Rapunzius from Trafalgar,' he continued. Such resounding foreign names help take people in too, you know, like pretty colours. 'If you take my tooth pills,' he went on, 'I can easily get rid of the pain, one of them will do the trick, at most two.' 'Please God you're right!' said the other rogue. So now the fine doctor Rapunzius took one of the red packets from his pocket and prescribed one pill, to be placed on the tongue and bitten on firmly. The customers at the other tables now craned their necks and one by one they came over to observe the miracle cure. You can imagine what happened! But no, the first bite seemed to do the patient no good at all, he gave a terrible scream. The doctor was pleased! They had, he said, got the better of the pain, and quickly he gave him the second pill to be taken likewise. Now suddenly the pain had all gone. The patient jumped for joy, wiped the sweat from his brow, though there was none there, and pretended to show his thanks by pressing more than a trifling sum into his saviour's hand. The trick was artfully done and had its desired effect. For all those present now wanted some of these excellent pills too. The doctor offered them at twenty-four kreuzers a packet, and they were all sold in a few minutes. Of course the two scoundrels now left separately one after the other, met up to laugh at the people's stupidity, and had a good time on their money.

The fools had paid dear for a few crumbs of bread! Even in times of famine you never got so little for twenty-four kreuzers. But the waste of money was not the worst part of it. For in time the pellets of breadcrumbs naturally became as hard as stone. So when a year later a poor dupe had toothache and confidently bit on a pill with the offending tooth, once and then again, just imagine the awful pain that he had got himself for twenty-four kreuzers instead of a cure!

From this we can learn how easy it is to be tricked if you believe what is told you by any vagrant whom you meet for the first time in your life, have never seen before and will never see again. Some of you who read this will perhaps be thinking: 'I was once silly like that too and brought suffering on myself!'

Remember: Those who can, earn their money elsewhere

and don't go around villages and fairs with holes in their stockings, or a white buckle on one shoe and a yellow one on the other.

A Short Stage

The postmaster told a Jew who drove up to his relay station with two horses, 'From here on you'll have to take three! It's a hard pull uphill and the surface is still soft. But that way you'll be there in three hours.' The Jew asked, 'When will I get there if I take four?' 'In two hours.' 'And if I take six?' 'In one hour.' 'I'll tell you what,' said the Jew after a while, 'Harness up eight. That way I shan't have to set off at all!'

Strange Reckoning at the Inn

Sometimes a cheeky trick comes off, sometimes it costs you your coat, often your skin as well. But in this case it was only coats. One day, you see, three merry students on their travels didn't have a brass farthing left between them, they had spent everything on a good time, but nevertheless they went into another inn intending to leave without sneaking out by the back door, and it suited them fine that they found only the landlord's nice young wife inside. They ate and drank merrily and talked very learnedly about the world being many thousands of years old and how it would last as long again, and how each year, to the day and the hour, everything that happened came to pass as it had done on that day and at that hour six thousand years before. Eventually one of them turned to the landlady, who was sitting on one side by the window knitting and listening attentively, and said, 'That's how it is, ma'am, we've had to learn that from our learned tomes.' And one had the impudence to assert that he just about remembered their being there six thousand years ago, and he remembered the landlady's pretty friendly face very well indeed. They carried on talking for some time, and the more the landlady seemed to believe everything they said the more the young gadabouts tucked into the wine and the meat and a fistful of pretzels, and in the end their bill stood chalked up at five guilders and sixteen kreuzers. They had eaten and drunk their fill, and now they came out with the trick they had planned.

'Ma'am,' said one, 'this time we are short of money, for there are so many inns on the road. But since we know you're a clever woman we hope that as old friends we can have credit here, and if you agree, in six thousand years' time when we come again we'll pay our old bill together with the new one.' The sensible landlady was not upset by that, it was fine by her, she was delighted that the young gentlemen were well served. But before they had noticed her move she was standing in front of the door and was asking the gentlemen kindly just to settle now the bill of five guilders and sixteen kreuzers that they owed from six thousand years ago, since, as they said, everything that happened now was an exact repetition of what had taken place before. Unfortunately just at that moment the village mayor came in with a couple of sturdy men to enjoy a glass of wine together. That didn't suit our gay young dogs at all! For now the official verdict was pronounced and carried out: you had to give it to someone who had allowed credit for six thousand years! The gentlemen were therefore to pay their old debt immediately or leave their newish overcoats as a pledge. They were obliged to take the second option, and the landlady promised to return their coats in six thousand years' time when they came again with a bit more money.

This took place in 1805 on the 17th of April in the inn at Segringen.

Unexpected Reunion

At Falun in Sweden, a good fifty years ago, a young miner kissed his pretty young bride-to-be and said, 'On the feast of Saint Lucia the parson will bless our love and we shall be man and wife and start a home of our own.' 'And may peace and love dwell there with us,' said his lovely bride, and smiled sweetly, 'for you are everything to me, and without you I'd sooner be in the grave than anywhere

else.' When however, before the feast of Saint Lucia, the
parson had called out their names in church for the
second time: 'If any of you know cause, or just hindrance,
why these two persons should not be joined together in
holy Matrimony' – Death paid a call. For the next day
when the young man passed her house in his black miner's
suit (a miner is always dressed ready for his own funeral),
he tapped at the window as usual and wished her good
morning all right, but he did not wish her good evening.
He did not return from the mine, and in vain that same
morning she sewed a red border on a black neckerchief
for him to wear on their wedding day, and when he did
not come back she put it away, and she wept for him, and
never forgot him.

In the meantime the city of Lisbon in Portugal was
destroyed by an earthquake, the Seven Years War came
and went, the Emperor Francis I died, the Jesuits were
dissolved, Poland was partitioned, the Empress Maria
Theresa died, and Struensee was executed, and America
became independent, and the combined French and
Spanish force failed to take Gibraltar. The Turks cooped
up General Stein in the Veterane Cave in Hungary, and
the Emperor Joseph died too. King Gustavus of Sweden
conquered Russian Finland, the French Revolution came
and the long war began, and the Emperor Leopold II too
was buried. Napoleon defeated Prussia, the English bom-
barded Copenhagen, and the farmers sowed and reaped.

The millers ground the corn, the blacksmiths wielded their hammers, and the miners dug for seams of metal in their workplace under the ground.

But in 1809, within a day or two of the feast of Saint John, when the miners at Falun were trying to open up a passage between two shafts, they dug out from the rubble and the vitriol water, a good three hundred yards below ground, the body of a young man soaked in ferrous vitriol but otherwise untouched by decay and unchanged, so that all his features and his age were still clearly recognizable, as if he had died only an hour before or had just nodded off at work. Yet when they brought him to the surface his father and mother and friends and acquaintances were all long since dead, and no one claimed to know the sleeping youth or to remember his misadventure, until the woman came who had once been promised to the miner who one day had gone below and had not returned. Grey and bent, she hobbled up on a crutch to where he lay and recognized her bridegroom; and, more in joyous rapture than in grief, she sank down over the beloved corpse, and it was some time before she had recovered from her fervent emotion. 'It is my betrothed,' she said at last, 'whom I have mourned these past fifty years, and now God grants that I see him once more before I die. A week before our wedding he went under ground and never came up again.' The hearts of all those there were moved to sadness and tears when they saw the former bride-to-be as an old woman whose beauty and strength had left her, and the groom still in the flower of his youth; and how the flame of young love was rekindled in her breast after fifty years, yet he did not open his mouth to smile, nor his eyes to recognize her; and how finally she, as the sole relative and the only person who had claim to him, had the miners carry him into her house until his grave was made ready for him in the churchyard.

The next day when the grave lay ready in the church-yard and the miners came to fetch him she opened a casket and put the black silk neckerchief with the red stripes on him, and then she went with him in her best Sunday dress, as if it were her wedding day, not the day of his burial. You see, as they lowered him into his grave in the churchyard she said, 'Sleep well for another day or a week or so longer in your cold wedding bed, and don't let time weigh heavy on you! I have only a few things left to do, and I shall join you soon, and soon the day will dawn.

'What the earth has given back once it will not withhold again at the final call', she said as she went away and looked back over her shoulder once more.

The Sly Pilgrim

A few years ago an idler roamed around the countryside pretending to be a pious pilgrim, saying he came from Paderborn and was making for the Holy Sepulchre in

Jerusalem, and already at the Coach and Horses in Mül-
heim he was asking, 'How far is it to Jerusalem now?'
They told him, 'Seven hundred hours. But you'll save a
quarter of an hour if you take the path to Mauchen.' So
he went by way of Mauchen to save himself a quarter of
an hour on his long journey. That wasn't such a bad idea.
You must not scorn a small gain or a bigger one won't
come your way. You more often get a chance to save or
make threepence than a florin. But eight threepennies
make a florin, and if on a journey of seven hundred hours
you can save a quarter of an hour every five hours, over
the whole journey you will save – now, who can work that
out? How many hours? But that wasn't how our supposed
pilgrim saw it! Since he was only after an easy life and a
good meal he didn't care which way he went. As the old
saying goes, a beggar can never take the wrong turning,
it's a poor village indeed where he can't collect more than
the cost of the shoe leather he has worn out on the road,
especially if he goes barefoot. Yet our pilgrim intended
to get back as soon as he could to the main road where
he'd find rich people's houses and good cooking. For this
rascal wasn't content, as a true pilgrim should be, with
common food given in compassion by a pious hand, he
wanted nothing but nourishing pebble soup! You see,
whenever he saw a nice inn by the road, for instance the
Post House at Krozingen or the Basel Arms at Schliengen,
he would go in and very humbly and hungrily ask for a
nice soup made of pebbles and water, in God's name, he

had no money. And when the innkeeper's wife took pity on him and said, 'Pious pilgrim, pebbles are not easy to digest!', he said, 'That's just it! Pebbles last longer than bread and it's a long way to Jerusalem. But if you were to give me a little glass of wine too, in God's name, it would help me digest them.' Now if she said, 'But good pilgrim, a soup like that won't give you any strength at all!' then he replied, 'Well, if you use broth instead of water then of course it would be more nourishing.' And when she brought him his broth and said, 'The bits at the bottom are still a bit hard, I'm afraid,' then he'd say, 'You're right, and the broth looks a little thin. Would you have a couple of spoonfuls of vegetables to add to it, or a scrap of meat, or maybe both?' If now the innkeeper's wife still felt sorry for him and put some meat and vegetables in the bowl, he said, 'God bless you! Now just hand me a piece of bread and I'll tuck into your soup!' Then he would push back the sleeves of his pilgrim's habit, sit down and set to work with relish, and when he had eaten the last crumb of bread, drained the wine, and finished the last morsel of meat and vegetables and the last drop of broth, he would wipe his mouth on the tablecloth or his sleeve, or perhaps he wouldn't bother, and he'd say, 'Missus, your soup has strengthened me as a good soup should, what a shame I can't find room for the nice pebbles now! But put them by, and when I come back I'll bring you a holy conch from the seashore at Ascalon or a Jericho rose.'

The Commandant and the Light Infantry in Hersfeld

In the last campaign in Prussia and Russia when the French Army and a large part of the allied troops were in Poland and Prussia, a contingent of the Baden Light Infantry was in Hessen and stationed at Hersfeld. For the Emperor had taken that state at the beginning of the campaign and stationed troops there. The inhabitants who preferred the way things had been before defied the new order and there were several acts of lawlessness, particularly in the town of Hersfeld. In one incident a French officer was killed. The French Emperor was engaged face to face with great numbers of the enemy and couldn't allow hostilities behind his back or let a spark spread into a great fire. The unfortunate people of Hersfeld thus had cause to regret their rashness. For the Emperor ordered the town to be looted, set alight at each corner and burnt to the ground.

This town of Hersfeld has many factories and thus many rich inhabitants and fine buildings; and all of us with a heart can understand how its unfortunate people, those fathers and mothers with families, felt when they heard the dreadful news. The poor whose possessions could be carried off in one pair of arms were just as much affected as the rich whose goods couldn't all be loaded on a train of wagons. Great houses on the town square and small dwellings in the alleyways are all the same when burnt to the ground, just like rich and poor in the graveyard.

But the worst didn't happen. The French Commandant in Kassel and Hersfeld interceded and the punishment was reduced. Only four houses were to be burnt down, and that was lenient. But the plundering was to take place as ordered, and that was hard enough. The wretched townsfolk, hearing this latest decision, were so cowed and robbed of all presence of mind that the benevolent Commandant himself had to urge them, instead of weeping and pleading in vain, to remove their most precious possessions in the short time that was left. The dreadful hour arrived, the drums sounded over the wails of anguish. The soldiers hurried to their place of assembly through the crowds fleeing in despair. Then the stalwart Commandant of Hersfeld stood before the ranks of the infantry, and first he painted a vivid picture of the sad fate of the townspeople, then he said, 'Men, you now have permission to loot! Those who wish to take part, fall out!' Not one man moved. Not a single one! The order was repeated. Not one pair of boots stirred, and if the Commandant had intended the town to be plundered he would have had to do it himself. But no one was more pleased than he was that things turned out as they did, that is easy to tell. When the townsfolk learnt this, it was as if they woke from a bad dream. No one can describe their joy. They sent a delegation to the Commandant to thank him for his kindness and magnanimity, and offered him a handsome gift to mark their gratitude. Who knows what they might not have done! But the Commandant refused and said he wouldn't be paid for a good deed.

This happened in Hersfeld in the year 1807, and the town is still standing.

A Poor Reward

When in the last Prussian war the French came to Berlin where the King of Prussia resides, a great deal of the royal property as well as other people's was taken and carried off or sold. For war brings nothing, it only takes. Much was claimed as booty, however well it was hidden they found it, but not everything. A large store of royal building timber remained undiscovered and untouched for some time. But eventually a rascal among the king's own subjects thought, there's a fair penny to be made here, and with a smirk and a wink he went to tell the French commandant what a lovely stack of oak and pine logs was still at such and such a place, and it was worth a few thousand guilders. But the French commandant paid him badly for this betrayal and said, 'Just you leave those fine logs where they are! There's no call to deprive the enemy of his most basic needs. For when your king returns he will need timber for new gallows for trusty subjects like you!'

Your Family Friend can only applaud that, and he would make a present of a few logs from his own coppice if they were needed.

A Curious Ghost Story

Last autumn a gentleman was travelling through Schliengen, a nice little place. And as he was walking up the hill to spare the horses he told a man from Grenzach the following story of what had happened to him.

Six months earlier this gentleman was on his way to Denmark, and late one evening he arrived in a village with a fine mansion on a hill outside, and he wanted to stay the night. But the innkeeper said he had no room, there was a hanging the next day and three hangmen were staying with him. So the gentleman replied, 'Then I'll ask up there in the big house. The owner, the governor or whoever he is, will take me in and find a spare bed for me.' The innkeeper said, 'There are plenty of fine beds with silk hangings up there all ready made up, and I'm in charge of the keys. But I wouldn't advise you to go there! Three months ago the lord and the lady and the young master went away on a long journey, and since then the mansion house has been haunted by ghosts. The steward and the servants had to leave, and all the others who have been to the house never went back a second time.' Our stranger smiled. For he was a plucky man who wasn't afraid of ghosts, and he said, 'I'll risk it!' Despite all the innkeeper's objections he had to hand over the key, and after the traveller had put together what was needed to pay a visit on ghosts he went to the mansion with his servant who was travelling with him.

Once inside he didn't undress or get ready for bed, but waited to see what happened. He put two lights to burn on the table and a pair of loaded pistols next to them, and to pass away the time he picked up the Rhinelanders' Family Friend, bound in gold paper, which was hanging by a red silk ribbon under the mirror in its frame on the wall, and looked at the nice pictures. For a long time nothing happened. But when midnight stirred in the church tower and the clock struck twelve, and a rainstorm was passing over the house and large drops were beating against the window, there were three loud knocks on the door and a ghastly apparition with black squinting eyes, a nose half a yard long, gnashing teeth, a beard like a goat and hair all over its body came into the room and said in a horrible growl: 'I am the lord Mephistopheles. Welcome to my palace! Have you said your goodbyes to your wife and children?' The visitor felt a cold shiver run up from his big toes over his back and up under his nightcap, and his poor servant was in a worse state still. But when this Mephistopheles came towards him, scowling dreadfully and stepping high as if he was crossing a floor of flames, the unfortunate gentleman thought: in God's name, this is the test! And he stood up boldly and pointed his pistol at the monster and said, 'Halt, or I'll shoot!' Not every ghost can be stopped like that, for even if you pull the trigger it doesn't go off, or the bullet flies back and hits you instead of the target. But Mephistopheles raised his first finger in warning, turned slowly on his heels and strode away just as he had come. Now when our traveller saw that this devil had respect for gunpowder, he thought, 'There's no danger now!', picked up a light in his free hand and followed the ghost cautiously along the passage; and his servant who was standing behind him ran for all he was worth out of this blessed place and down to the village, thinking he'd sooner spend the night with the hangmen than with spooks.

But suddenly in the passage the ghost disappeared from under the eyes of its plucky pursuer just as if it had gone through the floor. And when the gentleman went on another few paces to see where it had gone, all at once there was no floor under his feet and he fell down through a hole towards a flaming fire, and he himself thought he was on the way to hell. But after dropping about ten feet he found himself lying unharmed on a heap of hay in a cellar. And six weird fellows were standing around the fire, that Mephistopheles with them. All sorts of strange implements were piled up around them, and two tables stood heaped with shining thalers, each one more lovely than the other.

Now the stranger knew what was going on. For this was a secret band of forgers, all with blood running in their veins. They had taken advantage of the owner's absence and set up their mint in his mansion, and some of them were probably servants of the house who knew their way about; and to make sure they were not disturbed and discovered they wailed like ghosts, and anyone who came to the house was so frightened he never came back to take a second look. Yet the plucky traveller now had cause to regret his lack of prudence in not listening to the innkeeper's warnings. For he was pushed through a narrow opening into a small dark room and could hear them deciding his fate: 'The best thing is to kill him!' said one. But another said, 'First we must question him, find out who he is and where he's from.' When they then learnt he was a man of consequence and on his way to Copenhagen to see the king they looked at each other wide-eyed. And when he was back in the dark storeroom they said, 'This is a bad business. For if he's missed and they find out from the innkeeper that he came here and didn't leave, the hussars will come overnight and fetch us out, and there's plenty of hemp in the fields this year, so hangmen's nooses come cheap.' So they told their prisoner they would let him go if he swore an oath not to betray them, threatening they would have him watched in Copenhagen. And he had to tell them on oath where he lived. He told them, 'Next to the Green Man, on the left in the big house with green shutters.' Then they poured him some Burgundy wine and he watched them coining their thalers until it was light.

When the morning light shone down through the gratings, and they heard the sound of whips on the road and the cowherd blowing his horn, the traveller took leave of his night-time companions, thanked them for having him and went gaily back to the inn, quite forgetting that he had left his watch and pipe and the pistols behind in the mansion. The innkeeper said, 'Thank God you're back, I didn't get a wink of sleep! How did you get on?' But the traveller thought, an oath is an oath, and you mustn't take God's name in vain to save your life. So he said nothing, and as the bell was ringing and the wretched malefactor was being led out everyone ran off to watch. He said nothing in Copenhagen either, and almost forgot the incident himself.

A few weeks later, however, he received a parcel by the post, and in it were a pair of expensive new pistols inlaid with silver, a new gold watch set with diamonds, a Turkish pipe with a gold chain and a silk tobacco-pouch embroidered with gold, and in the pouch was a note. It said, 'We are sending you this to make up for the fright we gave you and to thank you for keeping quiet. It's all over now, and you can tell anyone you like.' So the traveller told the man from Grenzach, and it was that same gold watch that he took out at the top of the hill to check that the clock at Hertingen was striking noon on time, and later on in the Stork in Basel a French general offered him seventy-five new doubloons for it. But he wouldn't part with it.

One Word Leads to Another

A rich man in Swabia sent his son to Paris to learn French and a few manners. After a year or more his father's farmhand came to see him. The son was greatly surprised and cried out joyfully, 'Hans, whatever are you doing here? How are things at home, what's the news?'

'Nothing much, Mr William, though your fine raven copped it two weeks ago, the one the gamekeeper gave you.'

'Oh, the poor bird,' replied Mr William. 'What happened to it?'

'Well, you see, he ate too much carrion when our fine horses died one after the other. I said he would.'

'What! My father's four fine greys are dead?' Mr William asked. 'How did that happen?'

'Well, you see, they were worked too hard hauling water when the house and the barns burned down, and it did no good.'

'Oh no!' exclaimed Mr William, horrified. 'Our house burnt down? When was that?'

'Well, you see, nobody thought of a fire when your father lay in his coffin. He was buried at night with torches. A small spark soon spreads.'

'That's terrible news!' exclaimed Mr William in his distress. 'My father dead? And how is my sister?'

'Well, you see, your late father died of grief when the young Miss had a child and no father for it. It's a boy.

'There's nothing much else to tell,' he added.

A Bad Bargain

In the great city of London and round about it there are an extraordinary number of silly fools who take a childish delight in other people's money or fob watches or precious rings and don't rest until they have them for themselves. Sometimes they get them by cunning and trickery, but more often by fearless assault, sometimes in broad daylight on the open road. Some of them do well, others don't. The London jailors and executioners can tell a few tales about that! One day, however, a strange thing happened to a certain rich and distinguished man. The King and many other great lords and their ladies were gathered on a lovely summer's day in a royal park where the winding paths led to a wood in the distance. Crowds of other people were there too, they didn't think their journey or their time wasted if they could see that their beloved King and his family were happy and well. There was food and drink, music and dancing. There were walks to be taken in pairs or alone along the inviting paths and between scented rose bushes. A man, well-dressed so that he appeared to be one of the company, took up his stand with a pistol under his coat by a tree at a secluded spot where the park bordered on the wood, waiting for someone to come his way. And someone did come, a gentleman with a ring sparkling on his finger, a tinkling watch chain, diamonds in his buckles, and a ribbon and a star on his breast. He was strolling in the cool shade and thinking of nothing in particular. And while he was thinking of nothing in particular the fellow behind the tree stepped out, bowed low, pulled his pistol from under his coat, pointed it at the gentleman's breast and asked him politely to keep quiet, no one need know about their conversation! You can't help feeling uneasy when a pistol is aimed at you, you can never be sure what's in it! The gentleman very sensibly thought: better your money than your life, better lose a ring than a finger! and he promised to keep quiet.

'Now, Your Honour,' said this fellow, 'would you part with your two gold watches for a good price? Our schoolmaster adjusts the clock every day, so we can never be sure of the right time, and you can't see the figures on the sundial.' The gentleman had no choice, he was obliged to sell his watches to the scoundrel for a few pence, hardly the price of a glass of wine. In this way the rascal bought his ring and his buckles and the decorations off his breast, one after another and each for a paltry sum, with the pistol in his left hand all the time. When at last the gentleman thought, now he'll let me go, thank God!, the rogue began again.

'Your Honour, since we do business so easily, why don't

you buy some of my things from me?' The gentleman thought, I must grin and bear it, that's the expression, and said, 'Show me what you have!' The fellow took a collection of trinkets from his pocket, things he had bought at a tuppenny stall or filched from somewhere, and the gentleman had to buy them all from him, one after the other, none of them cheap. Eventually the rogue had nothing left but the pistol, but seeing that the gentleman still had a couple of lovely doubloons in his green silk purse he said, 'Sir, won't you buy this pistol of mine with what's left in your purse? It's made by the best gunmaker in London and it's worth two doubloons of anyone's money!' The gentleman was surprised. 'This robber's an idiot!' he thought, and bought the pistol. When he had bought it from the robber he turned the tables on him and said: 'Hands up, my fine friend, and do as I tell you, keep walking in front of me or I'll blow your brains out!' But the rogue darted off into the wood. 'Go ahead and shoot, Your Excellency,' he said, 'it's not loaded!' The gentleman pulled the trigger, and in fact it didn't go off. He pushed the ramrod into the barrel, there was no trace of powder. By now the thief was well away into the wood; and the distinguished Englishman walked back, red in the face at being frightened by an empty threat, and he had something to think about now.

A Secret Beheading

Whether or not on that morning of 17 June that year the executioner at Landau said the Lord's Prayer with proper devotion and its 'Lead us not into temptation but deliver us from evil' – that I don't know. But a delivery came, a note posted from Nancy, and if he hadn't said his prayers, then it arrived on just the right day. The note said: 'Executioner at Landau, come to Nancy straight away and bring your big sword. You will be told what to do and paid well.' A coach was waiting outside. 'It's my job', thought the executioner and got into the coach. When he was still one hour this side of Nancy, it was evening already and the sun was setting among blood-red clouds, the driver drew up, saying, 'It will be fine again tomorrow', when suddenly three strong armed men were standing by the road, climbed in beside the executioner and promised that he wouldn't come to any harm, 'But you must let us blindfold you!' And when they had put the blindfold over his eyes they said, 'Driver, drive on!' The coachman drove on, and it seemed to the executioner that he was taken a good twelve hours further, and he had no way of telling where he was. He heard the midnight owls; he heard the cocks crow; he heard the morning bells. Then without warning the coach stopped again. They took him into a house and gave him something to drink and a nice roll and sausage too. When he was strengthened by food and drink they led him on inside the same building, through several doors and up stairs and down, and then they removed his blindfold and he saw he was in a large room. It was hung all around with black drapes, and wax candles burnt on the tables. In the middle sat a woman on a chair with her neck bared and a mask over her face, and she must have been gagged, for she couldn't speak, only sob. Round the walls stood a number of gentlemen dressed in black and with black crape over their faces so that the executioner could not have recognized them if he had met them again an hour later. And one of them handed him his sword and ordered him to cut off the head of the woman sitting on the chair. The poor executioner's blood ran cold and he said they must excuse him: his sword was dedicated to the service of justice and he could not defile it with murder. But one of the gentlemen by the wall pointed a pistol at him and said, 'Get on with it! Do as we tell you or you'll never set eyes on the church tower at Landau again!' The executioner thought of his wife and children at home. 'If I've no choice,' he said, 'and I must shed innocent blood, then on your head be it!' and with one blow he severed the poor woman's head from her body.

When it was done one of the men gave him a purse with two hundred doubloons. They put the blindfold over his eyes again and took him back to the coach he had come in. The men who had brought him there escorted him again. And when at last the coach drew up and they let him get out and remove the blindfold he was left standing where the three men had joined the coach, one hour this side of Nancy on the Landau road, and it was night. The coach sped off back.

That is what happened to the executioner at Landau, and Your Family Friend is not sorry that he can't say who that poor soul was who had to take such a bloody way to life everlasting. No, nobody found out who she was, what sin she had committed, and nobody knows where she is buried.

The Fake Gem

Outside the Butcher's Gate at Strassburg there is a pleasant garden where anyone can go and spend his money on decent pleasure, and there sat a well-dressed man drinking his wine like everyone else, and he had a ring with a precious stone on his finger and held it so it sparkled. So a Jew came up and said, 'Sir, you have a lovely gem in that ring on your finger, I wouldn't mind that myself! Doesn't it glitter like the Urim and Thummim in the breastplate of Aaron the priest?' The well-dressed stranger answered very curtly, 'The gem is a fake. If it weren't, it would be on someone else's finger, not mine!' The Jew asked to take a closer look at it. He turned it this way and that in his hand and bent his head to look at it from every angle. 'He says this stone is a fake?' he thought, and offered the stranger two new doubloons for the ring. But the stranger said quite angrily, 'Why do you think I'm lying? I told you, it's a fake!' The Jew asked permission to show it to an expert, and someone sitting close by said, 'I'll vouch for the Israelite, he'll know what the jewel is worth!' The stranger said, 'I don't need to consult anyone, the stone's a fake.'

While this was happening Your Family Friend was sitting at another table in the same garden with good friends of his, happily spending money on decent pleasure, and one of the company was a goldsmith who knows all about gems. He fitted a soldier who lost his nose at the battle of Austerlitz with a silver one and painted it skin colour, and it was a good nose. The only thing he couldn't do was breathe the breath of life into it. The Jew came over to this goldsmith. 'Sir,' he said, 'would you say this is a fake stone? Can King Solomon have worn anything more splendid in his crown?' The goldsmith, who was also something of a stargazer, said, 'It shines like Aldebaran in the sky all right. I'll get you ninety doubloons for this ring. If you come by it cheaper the profit is yours.'

The Jew went back to the stranger. 'Fake or not, I'll give you six doubloons!' and he counted them out on the table, sparkling new from the mint. The stranger put the ring back on his finger and said, 'I have no intention of parting with it. If it's such a good fake that you think it's real that doesn't make it worth any less to me,' and he put his hand in his pocket so that the eager Israelite could no longer see the stone. 'Eight doubloons.' 'No.' 'Ten doubloons.' 'No.' 'Twelve – fourteen – fifteen doubloons.' 'Very well,' said the stranger at last, 'if you won't leave me in peace and insist on being deceived at all costs! But I tell you, in front of all these gentlemen here, the stone is a fake, and I'll not say it isn't. For I don't want any trouble. You can have the ring, it's yours.'

Now the Jew took the ring joyfully over to the gold-smith. 'I'll come for the money tomorrow.' But the goldsmith, who had never been taken in by anyone, opened his eyes wide in amazement. 'My friend, this isn't the ring you showed me two minutes ago! This stone is worth twenty kreuzers at most. This is the sort they make in the glass works at Sankt Blasien!' For actually the stranger had in his pocket a fake ring which looked as good as the one that had first sparkled on his finger, and while the Jew was bargaining with him and his hand was in his pocket, he pushed the genuine ring off his finger with his thumb and slipped his finger into the fake, and that was the one he had given the Jew. At once the dupe shot back to the stranger as if fired on a rocket: 'Oh, woe, woe unto me! I have been tricked, the stone is a fake!' But the stranger said coldly and calmly, 'I sold it to you for a fake. These gentlemen here are witnesses. It's yours now. Did I talk you into buying it or did you talk me into selling it?' All those present had to admit, 'Yes, he told you the stone was a fake when he said you could have it!' So the Jew had to keep the ring and no further fuss was made of the matter.

How a Ghastly Story was Brought to Light by a Common or Garden Butcher's Dog

Two butchers out in their district buying in animals came to a village and split up, one went left past the Swan, the other right, and they said, 'We'll meet up again in the Swan.' But they never did meet up again. For one of them went with a farmer into his cowshed. The farmer's wife went as well, though she was doing the washing in the kitchen, and their child decided to follow too. The devil gave the woman a nudge: 'Look at that belt full of money peeping out from under the butcher's shirt!' The woman gave her husband a wink, he gave her a nod, and they killed the poor butcher in the cowshed and hurriedly hid his body under some straw. The devil nudged the woman again: 'Look who's watching!' She looked round and saw the child. So, driven out of their minds by fear, they went back together into the house and locked the doors as if the enemy were near. Then the woman, whose heart was not just as black as sin but blacker and hotter than hell, said, 'Child, just look at you again! Come into the kitchen,' she said, 'I'll clean you up.' In the kitchen she pushed her child's head into the hot suds and scalded him to death. Now, she thought, there's no one to tell on us – but she didn't think of the murdered butcher's dog.

The murdered butcher's dog had run along a bit with the other butcher, and then, while the child was being boiled and then popped into the bread oven, the dog doubled back and picked up his master's scent, sniffed at the cowshed door, scratched at the door to the house, and knew that something was wrong. Off he ran at once, back into the village, looking for the other butcher. Soon he was whinging and whining and pulling at this butcher's coat, and the butcher, too, knew something was wrong. So he went with the dog back to the house, in no doubt that something dreadful had happened there. He beckoned over two men who were passing nearby. When the murderers heard the dog whining and the butcher shouting, they had nothing but the gallows before their eyes and the fear of hellfire in their hearts. The man tried to escape through the back window but his wife grabbed him by his coat and said, 'Stay here with me!' The man said, 'Come with me!' She answered, 'I can't, my legs won't move! Can't you see that ghastly figure outside the window, with its flaming eyes and fiery breath?' Meanwhile the door had been broken open. They soon found the two corpses. The criminals were taken and brought to court. Six weeks later they were put to death, their villainous corpses bound to the wheel, and even now the crows are still saying, 'That's tasty meat, that is!'

The Cunning Styrian

It was in Styria during the last war and some way off the main road, and a rich farmer was thinking: 'How can I keep my thalers and my dear little ducats safe in these evil times? I'm ever so fond of the Empress Maria Theresa, God bless her, and the Emperor Joseph, God bless him, and the Emperor Francis, God give him long life and health! And just when you think you have these dear sovereigns ever so safe and out of harm's way the enemy gets a whiff of them as soon as he sticks his nose into the village and takes them off prisoner to Lorraine or Champagne! It's enough to make a poor patriotic Austrian's heart bleed!' 'I've got it!' he said, 'I know what I'll do,' and in the dark moonless night he took his money out into the kitchen garden. 'The Seven Sisters will not betray me,' he said. Out in the garden he put the money straight down between the wallflowers and the sweet peas. Next to it he dug a hole in the path between the beds, threw all the soil on top of the coins and trampled on the beautiful flowers and the chard all around like someone treading down sauerkraut. The next Monday the Chasseurs were scouting all round the district, and on the Tuesday a patrol entered the village and went straight to the mill, and then with white elbows from the mill to our farmer. And an Alsatian brandished his sword and bawled at him, 'Out with your money, farmer, or say your last Our Father!' The farmer said they were welcome in God's name to take whatever they could find. He had nothing left, it had all gone yesterday and the day before that. 'You'll not find anything,' he said, 'you fine fellows!' When they found nothing except for a couple of coppers and a gilded threepenny piece with the image of the Empress Maria Theresa on it and a ring to hang it up by, the Alsatian said, 'Farmer, you've buried your money! Show us here and now where you buried your money or you'll leave for the hereafter without saying your last Our Father!' 'I can't show you it here and now,' said the farmer, 'I'm sorry, but you'll have to come with me out into the kitchen garden. I'll show you where it was hidden there and what happened. Our lords and masters, the enemy, were here before you, yesterday and the day before, and they found it and took the lot.' The Chasseurs saw how things looked in the garden, found everything just as the man said, and not one of them thought the money might be lying under the pile of earth, but each of them gazed into the empty hole and thought: 'If only I'd been here earlier!' 'And if only they hadn't ruined the wallflowers, and the chard as well!' said the farmer, and so he fooled them and all those who came after them, and so it was that he saved the whole family of archdukes, the Emperor Francis, the Emperor Joseph, the Empress Maria Theresa, and Leopold the First, the Most Blessed of All, and kept them safe in their own country.

A Report from Turkey

There is justice in Turkey. A merchant's man was over-taken on his journey by night and fatigue, tied his horse laden with precious goods to a tree not far from a guard-house, lay down under the shelter of the tree and went to sleep. Early next day he was woken by the morning air and the quails calling. He had slept well, but his horse had gone.

So he rushed off to the governor of the province, Prince Carosman Oglu he was called and he was staying nearby, and complained that he had been robbed. The prince cut the hearing short: 'So close to the guardhouse! Why didn't you ride on another fifty yards, then you would have been safe! It's your own stupid fault!' But then the merchant's man said, 'O just prince, should I have feared to sleep in the open in a land where you rule?' That pleased the Prince Carosman, and it annoyed him too. 'Drink a little glass of Turkish brandy tonight,' he said to the merchant's man, 'and sleep under the same tree again.' The man did just as he was told. The next morning when he was woken by the morning air and the quails calling he had slept well again, for the horse was standing there tethered at his side together with all the precious goods, and in the tree hung a dead man, the thief, who never saw the sun rise again.

They do say there are trees enough in most parts, big ones and little ones.

The Lightest Death Sentence

People have said it's the guillotine. But it isn't, you know! A man who had done much for his country and was highly thought of by its ruler was sentenced to death for a crime he'd committed in a fit of passion. Petitions or prayers were no use. But since he was otherwise highly regarded by the ruler, he, the prince, let him choose how he would like to die: he was to die in whatever way he chose. So the chief secretary came to him in prison: 'The prince has determined to show you mercy. If you wish to be put to death on the wheel you shall be put on the wheel; if you wish to be hanged he will have you hanged – there are already two up on the gallows but everybody knows there's room for three at a time. If, however, you would rather take rat poison there is some at the chemist's. For whatever kind of death you choose the prince says it shall be yours. But, as you know, die you must!' The criminal replied, 'If I really must die, then death on the wheel can be bent to suit one's taste, and hanging can be turned to suit one's inclination if the wind lends a hand. But you haven't got the point! For my part I have always thought that death from old age is the easiest way, and since the prince leaves the choice to me I'll choose it and no other!'

And that was his final decision, he wouldn't be talked out of it. So they had to let him go free and live on until he died of old age. For the prince said, 'I gave my word and I'll not break it.'

This little story comes from our mother-in-law who doesn't like to let anyone die if she can possibly help it.

A Stallholder is Duped

A rouble is a silver coin in Russia, worth a bit less than two guilders, whereas an imperial is a gold coin and worth ten roubles. So you can get a rouble for an imperial, for instance if you lose nine roubles at cards, but you can't get an imperial for a rouble. Yet a cunning soldier in Moscow said, 'Want to bet? Tomorrow at the fair I'll get me an imperial for a rouble.' The next day long rows of stalls were set out at the fair, the people were already standing at all the booths, admiring or finding fault, making bids and haggling, the crowd was walking up and down and the boys were saying hello to the girls, when up came the soldier with a rouble in his hand. 'Whose is this rouble? Is it yours?' he asked all the stallkeepers in turn. One of them who wasn't doing much business looked on for some time and then thought: if that money's too hot for you to hold I can warm to it! 'Over here, musketeer, it's my rouble!' The soldier said, 'If you hadn't shouted I would never have found you in the crowd,' and he handed him the rouble. The trader turned it one way and the other and tested its ring; it was a good one all right, and he put it in his purse. 'Now give me back my imperial, please!' said the musketeer. The trader said, 'I don't have any imperial of yours, I owe you nothing. You can have this stupid rouble back if you're playing a trick on me!' But the musketeer said, 'Hand over my imperial, this is no joke, I'm serious and can easily fetch a constable!' One thing led to another, a polite word to a defiant one, defiance to insults, and a crowd gathered around the stall like bees round a honey pot. Then something was burrowing its way through the throng. 'What's going on here?' said the police sergeant who had pushed through the crowd with his men. 'I said, what's all this?' The stallkeeper couldn't say much, but the musketeer had a good story to tell.

Less than a quarter of an hour before, he said, he had bought this and that from this man for one rouble. But when it came to paying he could find only a double imperial, nothing smaller, one his godfather had given him when he was enlisted. So he gave him the imperial until he came back with a rouble. When he came back with the rouble he couldn't find the right stall, so he asked at all the booths, 'Who do I owe a rouble?' And this man said it was him, and it was too, and he took the rouble but pretended he didn't have his imperial. 'Now will you agree to give it back?' The police sergeant questioned those around and they said: Yes, the musketeer asked at all the stalls whose rouble it was and this man said it was his, and took it too, and tested it to see if it was genuine. When the police sergeant heard that, he settled the matter: 'You've got your rouble, so give this soldier his imperial or we'll close down your stall and nail it up with you inside and leave you to starve to death!' Thus the police officer, and the trader it was who had to give the musketeer an imperial for a rouble.

Remember: Other people's property can eat into your own just as fresh snow swallows up the old.

Patience Rewarded

One day a Frenchman rode up on to a bridge over a stream, and it was so narrow there was scarcely room for two horses at once. An Englishman was riding up from the other side, and when they met in the middle neither of them would give way. 'An Englishman does not make way for a Frenchman!' said the Englishman. 'Pardieu,' said the Frenchman, 'My horse has an English pedigree too! It's a pity I can't turn him round and let you have a good look at his backside in retreat! But you could at least let that English fellow you're riding step aside for this English mount of mine. In any case yours seems to be the junior; mine served under Louis XIV in the battle of Kieferholz, 1702!'

But the Englishman was not greatly impressed. 'I have

all the time in the world!' he said. 'This gives me a chance to read today's paper until you are pleased to make way.' So with the coolness the English are famed for he took a newspaper from his pocket and opened it up and sat on his horse on the bridge and read for an hour, and the sun didn't look as if it would shine on this pair of fools for ever, it was going down quickly towards the mountains. An hour later when he had finished reading and was about to fold up the newspaper again he looked at the Frenchman and said, 'Eh bien?' But the Frenchman had kept his head too and replied, 'Englishman, kindly lend me your paper a while, so that I can read it too until you are pleased to make way.' Now, when the Englishman saw that his adversary was a patient man, he said, 'Do you know what, Frenchman? Come on, I'll make way for you!' So the Englishman made way for the Frenchman.

The Champion Swimmer

Before the war and all its afflictions when you could still cross freely from France to England and drink a glass or two in Dover or buy material for a waistcoat, a large mail boat sailed from Calais across the straits to Dover and back again twice a week. For the sea between those two countries is only a few miles wide at that point, you see. But you had to get there before the boat left if you wanted to sail on it. A Frenchman from Gascony seemed not to know that, for he came to Calais a quarter of an hour too late, just as they were shutting up the hens, and the sky was clouding over. 'Must I sit around here for a couple of days twiddling my thumbs? No,' he thought, 'I'd do better to pay a boatman a twelve-sous piece to go after the mail boat.' For a small craft can sail faster than the heavy mail boat, you understand, and will catch up with it. But when he was sitting in the open boat the boatman said, 'If I'd thought I'd have brought a tarpaulin!' For it began to rain, and how! Very soon it poured down from the night sky as if a sea up above was emptying itself into the sea below. But the Gascon thought, 'This is going to be fun!' 'Praise be,' said the boatman at last, 'I can see the mail boat.' And he pulled up alongside and the Gascon climbed aboard, and when he suddenly appeared through the narrow hatchway in the middle of the night and in the middle of the sea and joined the passengers on the ship they all wondered where he had sprung from, all on his own, so late and so wet. For on a ship like that it is like being in a cellar, you can't hear what is going on outside over the talk of the passengers, the sailors' shouts, the noise of the wind, the flapping sails and the crashing waves, and nobody had any idea it was raining. 'You look as if you've been keelhauled,' said one, 'pulled right under the ship from one side to the other, I mean.' 'Is that what you're thinking?' said the Gascon. 'Do you imagine you can go swimming and stay dry? If you can tell me how to do that I'll be glad to hear it, you see I'm

47

the postman from Oléron and every Monday I swim over to the mainland with letters and messages, it's quicker that way. But now I have a message to take to England. With your permission I'll join you, since I was fortunate enough to meet up with you. Judging from the stars it can't be far to Dover now.' 'You're welcome, fellow country-man,' said one (though he wasn't a fellow Frenchman but an Englishman) and blew a cloud of tobacco smoke from his mouth. 'If you have swum this far across the sea from Calais you must be a class above the black swimmer in London!' 'I'm not afraid of competition,' said the Gas-con. 'Will you take him on,' replied the Englishman, 'if I place a hundred louis d'or on you?' The Gascon said, 'You can bet I will!' It's the custom of rich Englishmen to bet with each other for large sums placed on men who excel at some physical activity. And so it was that this Englishman on the ship took the Gascon to London with him at his expense and had him eat and drink well so that he stayed fit and strong. 'My lord,' he said to a good friend of his in London, 'I have brought with me a swim-mer I found at sea. I bet you a hundred guineas he can beat your Moor!' His friend said, 'You're on!'

The next day they both appeared with their swimmers at an agreed spot on the river Thames, and hundreds of curious people had gathered there and they laid their bets too, some on the Moor, some on the Gascon, one shilling, or six shillings, one, two, five, twenty guineas, and the

Moor didn't give the Gascon much of a chance. But when they had both undressed the Gascon tied a little box to his body with a leather strap without saying why, as if that were quite normal. The Moor said, 'What are you up to? Have you learnt that from the champion jumper who had to tie lead weights to his feet when he was set to catch a hare and was afraid he would jump right over it?' The Gascon opened his box and said, 'I've only got a bottle of wine in here, a couple of saveloys and a small loaf of bread! I was going to ask you where you have your eats. For I shall swim straight down the river Thames into the North Sea and down the Channel into the Atlantic and on to Cadiz, and I suggest we don't call in anywhere on the way, for I have to be back in Oléron by Monday, that's the 16th. But tomorrow morning in Cadiz at the White Horse I'll order a good dinner for you so it will be ready by the time you arrive.' You, good reader, will hardly be imagining that he could escape that way! But the Moor was scared stiff. 'I can't compete against that amphibian!' he told his master. 'You can please yourself what you do!' And he got dressed again.

So the bet was over, the Gascon was given a handsome reward by the Englishman who had brought him there and everyone scoffed at the Moor. For although they must have seen that the Frenchman was only shamming, they were all amused by his bravado and the unexpected outcome, and for a month after that he was treated in the

49

inns and beerhouses by all those who had bet on him, and he admitted he had never been in the water in all his life.

The Weather Man

Just as a sieve-maker or a basket-weaver who lives in a small place cannot earn enough in his village or town to keep himself all year, but has to look for work and practise his craft in the countryside around, so our compasses-maker too does business away from home, and his trade is not in compasses but in knavish tricks that pay for a few drinks at the inn. Thus one day he appeared in Ober-ehingen and went straight to the mayor. 'Mr Mayor,' he said, 'could you do with different weather? I've seen how things are hereabouts. There's been too much rain on the bottom fields and the crops on the hill are behindhand.' The mayor thought that was easy to say but difficult to put right. 'Just so,' replied the compasses-maker, 'but that's my line of business! Didn't you know I'm the weather man from Bologna?' In Italy, he said, where the oranges and lemons grow, all the weather was made to order. 'You Germans are a bit behind in these matters.' The mayor was a good and trusting fellow and one of those who would like to get rich sooner rather than later. So he was attracted by the offer. But he also thought cau-tion was called for! 'As a test run,' he said, 'make it a clear sky tomorrow with just a few fluffy white clouds, sunshine all day with some streaks of vapour glistening in the air. Let the first yellow butterflies come out round midday, and it can be a nice cool evening!' The compasses-maker replied, 'I can't commit myself just for one day, Mr Mayor! It wouldn't cover my costs. I can only take on the job by the year. But then you'll have problems finding room to store your crops and the new wine!' When the mayor wanted to know how much he would charge for the year he was careful and didn't ask for payment in advance, only a guilder a day and free drinks until the matter was properly in hand, that could take at least three days – 'But after that a pint from each gallon of wine over what you press in your best years, and a peck from every bushel of fruit.' 'That's risnible,' said the mayor. He stood in awe of the compasses-maker and was using refined language, and people in his part of the country think it's refined to say 'risnible' for reasonable. But when he took pen and paper from the cupboard and was drawing up a schedule for the weather month by month the compasses-maker came up with a further complication: 'You can't do that, Mr Mayor! You will have to consult the people. The weather is a community matter. You can't expect every-one to accept your choice of weather.' 'You're right!' said the mayor. 'You're a sensible man.'

You, good reader, will have taken the measure of our compasses-maker and will have foreseen that the people could not agree on the matter. At their first meeting no decision was reached, nor even at the seventh, at the eighth hard words were spoken, and in the end a level-headed lawyer concluded that the best thing to do, to preserve peace and avoid strife in the community, was to pay the weather man off and send him packing. So the mayor summoned the compasses-maker. 'Here are your nine guilders, you mischief-maker, now make sure you leave before there's blood shed in the village!' The compasses-maker didn't have to be told twice. He took the money, left owing for about twelve pints of wine at the inn, and the weather stayed as it was.

Now then, as always the compasses-maker has much to teach us! In this case how good it is that up till now the supreme ruler of the world has always governed the weather according to his will alone. Even we calendar-makers, luminaries and the other estates of the realm are scarcely consulted and need lose no sleep on that score.

The Safest Path

Now and then even someone drunk has the occasional notion or good idea, as a fellow did one day who didn't take his usual path home from town but walked straight into the stream running alongside it instead. There he met a good man ready to offer a hand to a fellow, even a drunk one, in trouble. 'My good friend,' said the man, 'haven't you noticed you're in the water? The footpath's over here.' He too, replied the drinker, generally found it best to use the path, but explained that this time he had had one too many. 'And that's just why I want to help you out of the stream,' said the good man. 'And that's just why I want to stay in it,' replied the drinker. 'Because if I walk in the stream and fall, I fall on to the path, but if I fell when walking on the path, I'd fall into the stream.' And that's what he said, tapping his forehead with his index finger, as if to show that he still knew a thing or two that might not have occurred to anyone else, despite being a bit the worse for wear.